It's Raining Bubbles

It's Raining Bubbles

iUniverse books may be ordered through booksellers or by contacting:

iUniverse
1663 Liberty Drive
Bloomington, IN 47403
www.iuniverse.com
1-800-Authors (1-800-288-4677)

ISBN: 978-1-5320-8011-1 (sc)
ISBN: 978-1-5320-8012-8 (e)

Library of Congress Control Number: 2019914026

Print information available on the last page.

iUniverse rev. date: 10/31/2019

Rain, hail, sleet, and snow—these are all weather we know. But when something unexpected happens and it starts raining bubbles, what will the children do? What happens when the children try to touch the bubbles? Who is responsible for the bubbly weather? Children will relate to this charming story.

Dedication

For my sister Mila, who believed in me; for my editor, Keith
Gordon, who steered me in the right direction; for my students
over the last sixteen years, who have helped me to develop a deeper
passion for books; and for my Angels, who made it happen.

One day in a small land far way,
a town awoke to bubbles.

Bubbles bounced off rooftops and
landed on trees; they floated past traffic
lights and shimmered on leaves.

Bubbles stuck to pole lines,
tumbled on top of cars,

glided over apartment buildings, and
bounced around people's backyards.

News of the weather spread quickly around town; TV shows were interrupted as news got around.

Never had the weather triggered such attention. The story
made front page news; it deserved special mention.

Traffic that morning was nothing but bubbly bliss. The residents of this small town drove their cars at their own risk.

A steady stream of cars made their way up a steep hill.
The ground beneath them was slippery, then stilled.

A bubble landed on the neighborhood dog's tail. He whimpered he howled and started to growl. He tried to catch the bubble by chasing his tail, but the bubble went *Pop!* and he started to wail.

Children from everywhere came rushing outside to play.
They were so excited to see bubbles fall this way.

The children chased the bubbles down the street and around the block, only to hear the bubbles say, "Catch us if you can!" followed by *Pop! Pop! Pop!*

Children leaped in the air to catch the bubbles with one hand,
but the bubbles popped like bacon in a hot frying pan.

Others watched the bubbles as they fluttered to the ground.
There was a new-found joy with the bubbles all around.

Soon the residents of this small town discovered something new;
no longer did their faucets dispense water, but bubbles too!

Now at the beauty parlor there was no need for shampoo; bubbles from the faucet worked good as new. The bubbles from the faucet worked up more lather, and the customers agreed the bubbles went farther.

Then suddenly, a cloud of steam rose into the air; it stopped raining bubbles and the bubbles evaporated.

The following day the sky was a clear blue, and the children of this small town went off to school.

They chittered and chattered about the recent weather while the kindergarten students thought the sky was so clever.

Late that afternoon, around two thirty, students in gym class became hot and thirsty. They formed a line at the water fountain, but out of the faucet came bubbles as high as a mountain.

The children soon became hyper and unruly,
screaming and shouting and acting all perky.

The bubbles drifted throughout the school, inside
the classrooms and into the lunchroom.

Now the entire school was out of control! The principal, Mr. Suds, was soon out on patrol.

In his haste, he came rushing down the hall, but since
the floor was slippery he had a sudden fall.

His toupee slid off the right side of his head. His bald patch was showing and his face turned red.

He ordered the children to settle on down, but they couldn't stop giggling with this toupee on the ground.

Then all off a sudden, the sky turned blue, and bubbles started falling outside just like dew. All at once, the children ran outside. The falling bubbles were such a pleasant surprise.

Then a bubbly fairy appeared in the clouds with a wand in her hand, and she smiled pleasantly at the children all over the land. With a soft sweet voice, she said, "Children, children everywhere, I have some splendid news, I sent the bubbles down to keep you all amused.

Whenever you want more bubbles, just follow the bubbly rule: Slide to the left, slide to the right, move your hips from side to side, wave your hands up in the air, then shout out *Bubbles!* and bubbles will appear!

And when you want the bubbles to stop, twist to the ground, then to the top, and right away the bubbles will stop."

With no toupee and a speaker in his hand, Principal Suds
hatched one big plan. He twisted to the ground then to the
top, and just like magic, the bubbles suddenly stopped

He made an announcement to the entire school that raining
bubbles were now a part of the school rules. At recess time, the
students could play with bubbles if they were good and stayed
out of trouble. The students agreed to comply with the principal's
command, and from that moment on they had bubbles on demand.

Late that night when the town went to sleep,

the children dreamed of bubbles bouncing up and down their streets.